Peggy's Seaside Holiday

Nicholas Clifford

Peggy's Seaside Holiday
Copyright © 2021 by Nicholas Clifford

Tellwell Talent
www.tellwell.ca

ISBN
978-0-2288-5269-8 (Hardcover)
978-0-2288-5268-1 (Paperback)

Peggy's Seaside Holiday

There was once a girl called Peggy, who lived in a small apartment on the tenth floor of a tall red brick building.

When it was sunny, she liked to play in the park across the road, but it rained very often.

Mostly, Peggy would sit at the window, looking out at the skyscrapers towering into the clouds and dreaming of adventures in far-off places.

One day Peggy's parents told her that they were all going on a holiday to get away from the grey buildings and the rain for a while.

She was so excited. She rushed around, looking for her favourite clothes to put into her suitcase. It was dark by the time they had packed the car and set off. Peggy sat in the back, watching the houses and fields drift by in the moonlight.

Before long she fell fast asleep.

When Peggy awoke, she found herself in bed in a small white room, with sunlight streaming through the window. She could smell coffee from the kitchen and the sounds of toast being buttered.

Quickly, before anyone could hear that she was up, she slipped quietly out the front door.

Only a short way from the house was a beach, stretching far away. There was a light breeze blowing in from the sea and gentle waves were washing upon the white sand. Peggy saw some rocks in the distance and, wondering what curious things she might find in the rock pools, she hurried excitedly towards them.

Arriving at the rocks, Peggy found them not to be as she had expected. They were big and smooth and there were no rock pools to be seen. Disappointed, she turned to run back to the house for breakfast when she heard a deep rumbling sound. It seemed to be coming from one of the rocks. She pressed her ear to the stone and heard a faint voice. 'Help us,' it groaned. 'We're stuck.' 'Who are you?' asked Peggy, but there was no answer.

Wondering what to do, Peggy clambered up onto one of the big rocks and sat there, looking out to sea. Suddenly, there was a sound of bubbles and a very strange creature surfaced from the water. It was bright yellow, with a long snout and ridges along its back.

'Are you a sea monster?' asked Peggy, feeling a little worried.

'Why, no! ' the creature squeaked in a friendly voice. 'I'm a sea horse! My name's George.'

'Oh,' said Peggy. 'Do you know who is trapped in these rocks?.'

'No, I don't know anything about that! But if you're looking for answers to questions, Old Man Grouper is the one to ask. He's the wisest fish in these parts, old as the sea-hills. Hop on my back. We'll go and find him!'

Peggy climbed on the sea horse's back. Down into the sea they went. At first everything appeared blurry, but slowly her eyes became accustomed to the water. She was amazed at what she saw.

There were fish flashing past in every direction and giant crabs paraded along the sand of the sea floor. In the distance, sharks circled around an old shipwreck. George swam fast, his long tail beating the water rhythmically. Peggy held tightly to his ridged back. They headed towards a dark forest of kelp.

Deep in the kelp forest, they arrived at a clearing. There, chewing slowly on some weed, swam the biggest fish Peggy had ever seen.

'Hello, young George,' he boomed 'And who is this small person you've brought along to me?'

'I am Peggy,' she said timidly.

'If you please, Mr Grouper, do you know who is trapped in the rocks on the beach?'

Old Man Grouper opened his wide mouth and sighed deeply. 'It is the whales, my dear child. A very sad story indeed, but there is nothing to be done. That cruel Mrs Moray has cast a spell on them. She is not an eel to be reasoned with. I have tried many times to speak with her but she hides away in her cave.'

'But surely we have to try again?' cried Peggy. 'You may try, good child,' said the Grouper. 'Perhaps you may find a way to her cold heart, but be very careful and do not step inside her cave, or you may never get out! Good luck!' George swam down into the darkness. Peggy hugged her arms around his neck as the water became colder.

'Here we are!' he whispered as a glittering cave of green coral came into view.

Out of the dark caverns glided a long shape. 'Hellooooo' it hissed softly. 'Would you like to come inside my cave?'

'No thank you, Mrs Moray' replied Peggy firmly.

'We want you to release those whales on the beach.'

Mrs Moray snarled and her sharp white teeth glinted in the dark.

'Those nasty whales ate all my octopus. They deserve to stay there, for stealing my dinner.' 'But you can't just turn them into stone! What if the grandfather of whales promised to stop them eating any more octopus?'

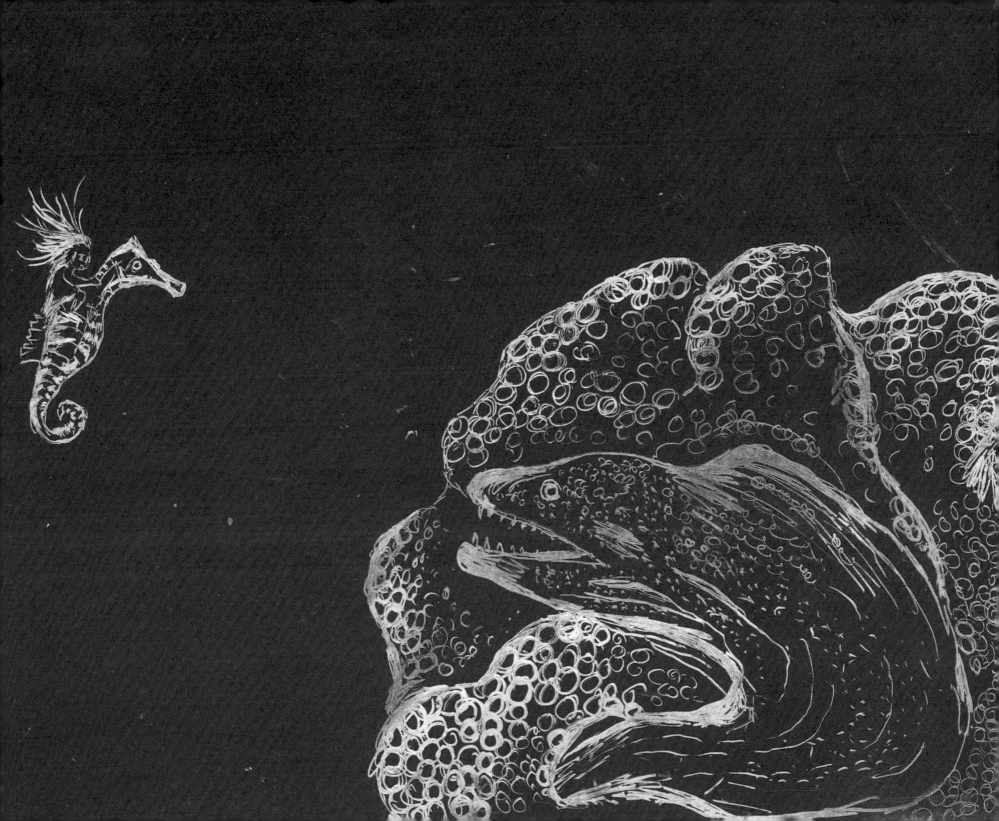

'I suppose I could release them, if it was promised and if you promise to come for dinner in my cave, little girl.' hissed Mrs Moray.'

Alright then,' said Peggy, crossing her fingers tightly behind her back, 'It's a deal.'

Off they swam again, out into the deep ocean. 'I hope we'll find the grandfather whale here' said George. 'He roams far and wide.'

In the distant water, Peggy could make out the shape of a small fish. 'Hello!' she called. ' Have you seen a whale?' The shape seemed to move slowly towards them, increasing in size. It got bigger and bigger and bigger, until it dwarfed Peggy and George.

'The grandfather whale' cried Peggy.

'Yes, little one?' it said, in a deep rumble like thunder.

'You must promise to stop eating Mrs Moray's octopus. Then she will release your friends from the beach!'

'Stop eating octopus? Then what shall we eat instead?' asked the whale.

'Well, couldn't you eat squid? It's almost the same. It even has more legs!' replied Peggy. 'Squid...oh. Well... I had never thought of that' said the grandfather whale, for although he was very big he was rather old and slow in his thoughts. 'Hmm. I don't see why not. Just hadn't occurred to me.'

'Quick!' ordered Peggy. 'Make the promise to Mrs Moray.'

The grandfather whale let out a series of sounds like a ship's fog horn, which echoed across the ocean. Then, faintly in reply, Peggy heard a hissing sound which she knew was Mrs Moray whispering her deep magic.

The water around them started to shimmer and sparkle. In the brightness Peggy and George saw the shapes of many whales appear. The spell was lifted and they were free again. They began to swim joyfully around the seahorse and his small passenger, swishing their broad tails and calling out in their thunderous voices. 'Thank you, Peggy!' they seemed to be saying. 'We won't forget you!'.

'Now quickly' squeaked George. 'Let's get you home, before Mrs Moray finds out!' With dazzling speed he raced through the water, up and up through the water until everything was a blur of blue.

Suddenly Peggy found herself back on the beach. The sun was shining and she felt the cool sea breeze on her damp clothes. Her parents were walking towards her. 'Come on Peggy, it's time for breakfast!' her mother called. She trotted towards them.

As she ran she thought she heard a faint squeak on the wind 'Goodbye Peggy! See you again!'

The end

Lightning Source UK Ltd.
Milton Keynes UK
UKRC032107140922
408854UK00001B/6

* 9 7 8 0 2 2 8 8 5 2 6 8 1 *